NOW I CAN GO ON

Patricia Marie G

Copyright © 1987 by **Patricia Marie**

Patricia Marie G/Key to the Gate LLC

P.O. Box 1878

Bethany, Ok. 73008-1878

www.keytothegatellc.com

Cover design by: vikncharlie

Now I Can Go On 3rd edition

Patricia Marie G

13: 978-1-7321395-0-3

Dedication:

This book is dedicated to the one who brought me through so many dark nights. He gave me strength and hope. During the battles in my life, He never failed nor abandoned me. He will do the same for you. Simply take His outreached hand. His name is Christ Jesus.

Forward

I spent many nights as you are about to read in this book. This is only one of those nights.

It is written in the form of a physical battlefield. The story is real, simply on a different battlefield. It didn't take place in a building but outside in many areas. Battles involving, life and death.

The story takes multiple personalities placing each in this one night.

I was not in the military, yet I fought many battles for others freedom and healing. I have been a medic to the wounded.

I spent this night with a girl who tried to take her life. Many others are calling out in pain from various struggles, battles. By the Grace of God, I brought her and the others through.

The next day I walked into my house, drained. My home quiet, peaceful as I leaned back. I shut my eyes trying to rest. In my mind, the cries were being replayed. The battles took on a different battlefield. Thus this is what I saw and thought.

Cruel words also actions were the bullets that struck victims.

In life and war, the struggle to survive is real.

I have seen the battles of many as they fought their enemy of fears, drugs, alcohol, broken relationships. The list is endless.

The will to live is a powerful force. What we line up our will with is crucial to the outcome of any battle.

We must fight the real enemy, or we will have no real victories.

Often, we see someone as our enemy, yet the true enemy is within them. Within them from past or present hurt, fears. The real enemy takes on many disguises.

Fear is the doorman to imaginations as it closes the door to reality.

I have known many who felt they could go no further. These were broken people with great inner pain. Their thoughts ran deep within their minds.

The past can be a cruel taskmaster so dangerous to the present and future.

Self-worth must not be determined by the past failures or the false judgment of others.

Cruel words and deeds are like snipers bullets wounding, destroying someone's self-worth even their life. Shattered hopes and dreams I have seen in many faces after the cruelty of such abuse.

Isn't it true we are to be medics to the wounded not the destroyer of their soul? So many have almost destroyed the lives of others while wearing their self-righteous robes.

I truly believe when someone cries out, we are to pray, care.

Everyone wants to be the famous leader. The ones reaching out on a daily bases are more vital and honorable. Such givers of love for God have a special place in His heart.

We must lay down our weapons that can harm.

True some people are the abusers. We must pray first, react second, always cautious.

Some are not ready nor do not want help. Some are evil, but many broken people are not. I am not blind to that fact.

It is wrong to leave people in tears, looking away not wanting to see.

The abusers beat down what they know can exceed them. The only time they feel strong or in control is through the subjection of another. Subjection until the abused lose their own identity, thoughts, dreams.

Not all abusers are men, some are women as well, even teens.

Some abusers have a mental disease, so caution and prayer are vital always.

It is important to clear your path before you walk it through prayer. Also, place a hedge of Holy Angels around yourself and others. Pray the enemy's eyes be blinded to see ways of hurting the wounded. Everyone's heart turned unto God. God will rule over it all. Fear of the victims become powerless, and they find faith, healing. Victims always need faith that there is hope. The faith they can be healed and free.

Caution, notice your surroundings, be aware of the movements of people around you, and listening to voice tones. Left-handed people need to be approached differently because of their movements are so different than a right-handed person.

Do not let emotions drive you. Only do as you are positive God is sending you. It is the anointing that breaks the yoke.

THE NIGHT BEGINS

I have left the others for I desperately need time alone. It is quiet for a few moments. As I shut my eyes, I still see the pain in others. I hear their cries. I quickly opened my eyes to see something different.

The setting sun arrays the sky with many colors. A unique sunset is as unique as I know this night will be. The dawn opens the page of a brand new day. The sunset not only ends the day but brings in the night.

I looked upon the peaceful beauty of the heavens above. I longed for such peaceful serenity to array me. Deep within me, I felt rage over what I have seen going on. I need to take hold of something. I simply didn't know what it would be. Where can such peace and freedom be found in this craziness?

I came here to help others to know freedom. For so long I have done this. Have I lost my freedom as I the struggle to help them? What has it cost me for their freedom? What will the future cost be? I am not sure what those answers are. There is something within me that has always driven me to this. My mind and warrior side cannot turn away from the wounded. I keep telling myself I am tough but am I tough enough?

The wind rushed by me in a hurry as if like me, it has a destiny to meet. A destiny I don't know how to make any changes. I use to run with the wind from place to place. I never gave much thought to where it was taking me. I only thought about my need to be free. I guess I thought it was going to take me to a happy, peaceful place.

I am not feeling sorry for myself. Maybe my struggles have given me the strength I need to help others. I have been a natural born survivor. I have lived through many horrible battles in my own life. Something has always brought me through. I have felt there must be a God.

This night ahead had to be one of the darkest I have ever faced. I know I will not give in or surrender. I know those in this, will fight the best as they could.

For some reason, the enemy held off their worst attacks until the night hours.

You can feel the tension and fear in each person. They were all becoming drained from the battles. Their battles have been too many for too long. It has taken a toll on their mind, body, especially their soul.

There is one thing I have noticed; each is affected differently. They are all in this together but affected individually, revealing their strong and weak areas. It is amazing how it reveals how to reach each one.

Their faces, voice levels, and body language showed their fear for their survival and of those they called a friend.

Jason is a man of great fame and fortune. I nicknamed him, Performer. I have never seen any of his shows until now. Most the others said, "he was a great singer." They added, "he was also an excellent showman."

He is totally out of place here. He tries to keep others around. He is lost without his fans to encourage him on. His own self-confidence depends on their applause.

His parents are extremely wealthy. As his first cheering fans, they spoiled him.

I am truly amazed in a humorous way by him. The only value his fame has here is the men. He has to hit the ground with the rest of us. He has to weather dry or muddy. I have sat and laughed inside at him. He is such a pansy. You wouldn't believe his expressions in the mud. The whimpering, oh it is endless.

I have heard there is a price for fame and fortune. I think I now know the price.

I laughed while watching him. He looked over at me with a stern look. He told me, "I am a serious performer, not a comedian." I couldn't help but laugh as I told him, "yes you are a character for sure."

I am amused by him, but at the same time, I am concerned for him. I feel he would have more chance to survive if he had to before now.

I am not for sure how he ended up here. I honestly don't think he knows either. When I asked him, he snapped back at me; "I hope it isn't just to amuse you." I smiled when I replied, "well there are worst reasons." He stomped off, looked back at me mumbling. I do enjoy him. In this craziness he makes me smile even laugh.

Performer isn't used to someone not being impressed with his fame nor his fortune.

Outside of his fame, he has no common ground to communicate with others. Once the new wears off, he will have a difficult time. He can not relate or understand where they have been. Nor can he understand how to respond to what they talk about. He will be lost and alone, something he has never known. Or has he? It is easy to prejudge someone, isn't it?

I don't think all wealthy people think like him. To him, the poor are simply people with germs and bad clothing choices. Having limited choices, he has never known.

I don't think he has the inner strength nor the determination to come through this. If he does survive, I am sure he will come out a better person.

As for now, Performer complains all the time about his aching body. His clothes and shoes are definitely a great thing he has found to complain about also. Such a peacock.

Our company only has three officers left.

Wilson came from a long line of officers. He was merely playing follow the leaders.

He is trying to fit the mold, but man, he does not fit it.

I feel sorry for him, yet he scares me.

At one point in the heat of battle, it was horrid how he almost cost us our life. He came from the mold, but he doesn't have all the right ingredients.

It is sad these people didn't know soldiers are as important to the overall victory. Medics are vital.

What else could he do? They had their status symbol. We faced dangerous times with him as our leader.

Wilson has reached the edge of a break down many times in these battles. He darted around screaming crazy commands that made no sense. During those times we had to put our lives on the line to rescue him.

Maybe I am lucky after all no one expected me to fit into any mold of their making. The only thing expected of me is simply to be me.

I heard Wilson telling someone how his family enjoyed tea parties. He added how pleased they were with him carrying on the military family line.

They sit around in their tea parties talking about their status symbol. We are trying to live past Wilson's stupid, continuous speech and commands.

Do they even comprehend at all who he is actually? Oh, maybe it wouldn't matter or would it?

I don't feel he will make it through this. Sadly enough I am concerned how many he will take with him. Who knows maybe his blue blood will show through in time? I truly hope so.

Our second officer is Chase. He came from a long line of trouble. He only knew abuse and hunger. Due to his inner determination, he rose above all the horrid past.

Chase had a strength, survival awareness. Like myself, he watched body language, listened to voice levels. Survivors traits do watch others differently. Due to a comment he made I know he also watched if someone was right or left handed. I do that also. Left-handed people's movements are so different. A right-handed person should always be both aware and prepared to respond differently.

I have a common ground with him because we are similar in many ways. I believe he will survive at least I hope so. If he doesn't, well it would be a terrible loss. He cares for others in genuine ways. He thinks before he answers, weighing all options. He doesn't seek any personal glory.

I have no doubt Chase can help me bring the others through their battles. It is simply a matter if the egos of the other two officers will allow him to do so.

In the heat of battle, the egos of the other two officers got several wounded. Chase couldn't reason with them.

Ego and hunger for power are deadly to the innocent and can never be satisfied. They are driven by an monster force within them.

Our third officer is Bruce. He is nothing short of crazy for power and a control freak. The man is dangerous. He is right, no matter the cost. He has been willing to place others life at high risk to be right. Everyone is feeling the effects of his wrong decisions.

At first, pretty much everyone gave him a chance. He shoves his authority in everyone's face. Now no one has respect for him nor do they relate to him.

His demands are stupid. We have been ordered to lay our weapons down and stand to salute him. Commanded to do so with bullets flying. Such a demand for power is a creator of anger.

I overheard a few of the men talking about him. One said, "maybe Bruce will be captured." Another replied, "they would send him back with a note on him. It would read, do not allow this pompous jerk to end up with us again." They all laughed. "No doubt."

Larry loves all of this. He is built like a weightlifter. Larry is a crazy bear in a man's body.

He jumps in the middle of things laughing as if he is at a fun party. This is nothing short of one huge blast to him.

I would never want to be his enemy. He would be almost impossible to take down. Wild people have wild movement and aggression.

One of our men told me, "he was going to stay close to Larry. He was planning on making friends with him." He added, "a great idea, don't you think?"

I told him, "to a point it is but Larry would take you to places you will not want to go. Dangerous, unreasonable places, for sure. Do you want to go there? Do you think you could tell him no? I don't think you could."

Performer is complaining about the food. He repeats over and over; "I have never had to eat this way. I have never done without like I have to do now."

I started to ignore him than I realized, how could he understand until now?

I stopped, watched and paid attention to what he actually was saying. Maybe I can learn from him even gain new compassion myself.

Rich people bore me. I have seen them as only a plastic fork placed in fine china.

He had never experienced hunger. So how could he have compassion for the hungry? A hungry person sees and tastes food in a different way than those with a full stomach.

To experience some things first-hand can change a person's thinking and often even their heart. Take for example love. It is only a word unless you have felt it, have been overtaken by it. It is only a word otherwise. Maybe hunger has been simply a word to him.

Maybe it isn't his fault that he doesn't know the difference.

I thought at first he was going to be a complete burden. Now I wonder about that.

Surely I am not learning to like or appreciate this peacock.

Funny how life has an unexpected twist to it.

James built his whole life around his sweetheart. He leans back daydreaming about her. He has it bad. To him, she is nothing short of perfect. He showed me her picture. Man, she isn't pretty that I could see. To him she is awesome. Wow, it is proof no one sees things the same.

We listen, but we are sick of hearing about her. We understand his need to keep his mind on her for the inspiration. She keeps him hanging on.

I haven't found anything else important to him. I just let him continue to tell me about her. But man how many times can you hear the same story? It looks like I will learn the answer to that.

Love is good, but no way do I think it should be an obsession. Obsession is consuming of the victim. Both become victims, the obsessed and the one being obsessed about. They lose their real identity. How can she live up to or be as perfect as he believes her to be? Where in his story does she get to be who she is created to be? She is simply a human with strong and weak points.

What about him not determining his identity based on her. What a roller coaster ride that can be for anyone.

Thank God I have never loved like James. Nor have I allowed someone to demand or expect me to be a perfect robot. What happens when I feel too tired to amuse or build them up?

I never want to lose my identity nor capture another with unfair expectations. No stupid demands, just love them for who they are.

I enjoy watching a bird soar, flying free. I never want to capture it unto myself. To cage a bird cheats me out of enjoying its beautiful flight.

A bird's feathers come from within. Our growth to form who we are also comes from within.

Granted there are other things and people who affect our growth. We determine within ourself how much circumstances or others affect who we are. We must keep hold of who we choose to become.

James is only in his twenties. I wonder if some of his thinking maybe is his youth. Everything including first love is dramatic.

The sun is almost setting now. I truly wish I could stop the night. I wish I had an instant fix for the wounded, scared people. I do not.

I honestly do need more time before the battles intensify.

The bullets are increasing. Those wicked snipers are also increasing in their sneaky maneuvers.

Everyone is responding in the only way they know how. Everyone tries to look tough but I know inside they are afraid. Everyone but Patrick.

Patrick is different than anyone else here. He seems to know something we don't. He is always, I mean always showing a positive attitude. At times I felt like throwing something at him, but he would just think I wanted to play catch. That's simply the way he thinks. It's nothing short of weird.

I respect someone with a good attitude, but this man is made of iron. He is unaffected by what is going on around him. It isn't that he is unaware of what is going on. He is quiet and caring. I would never believe he doesn't care.

So odd, I have watched him in the heat of battle lay down his weapon. He would rush to the side of the wounded. He would kneel down beside those wounded. Encouraging each of them as they needed.

He brought them peace as he eased their pain. His caring kept them holding on.

All the wounded and frightened heard him pray for them.

He looks human, but he has something within him beyond that.

Many other times as I looked over at him, he had laid his weapon down. Instead, he was holding on a something on a chain. I have learned it is a cross.

I wish everyone would lay down their weapons of hate and abuse.

Many who never acted as if they had ever heard of a God. They also acted like they definitely never prayed to one suddenly cried out to Him. It isn't unusual in times like this.

Yankee is crude, cruel with his words and actions. Shoving others around, demanding his own way. I have seen him tear hurting people to shreds. He laughed as he pushed deep into their wounds. He makes it clear he doesn't care about anyone's feelings.

I can do without that type of person around me. Such people bring out a response in me to change their wicked ways.

I wish he would shut up for a while.

Yankee tries ripping Patrick every chance he gets. Attacking Patrick seems to be his point of getting up every morning.

I have closely watched Patrick. Patrick did not allow Yankee to control his emotions. Patrick kept control amazingly well. He was able to go on his way with a smile, caring for others.

I don't understand what is going on in his head. I find myself fascinated with Patrick. Was it his faith that carried him on in strength?

I believe there is a God. I have never been able to comprehend why or if He could care about me. Why would He? I tried to be a Christian, but no way could I measure up. I guess I thought I couldn't measure up to God's standards. Maybe I should have tried harder.

They preached, hell and damnation. Patrick draws others to God with his concern and kindness. No one can reject it. Compassion and mercy that he gave are needed throughout this world.

Christians are more watched than anyone else, even more than politicians. I used them a few times for a cop out myself. I find no way I can use Patrick as a cop out.

Like a multitude of others. I know, I was trying to cover up my feelings of not being good enough.

It is sure easier to be a sinner than to face the fact that you're no saint.

He quietly draws you to his God. I thought about the cross he wears.

Why did Jesus do it? Was he simply stuck in it as we are now? Why?

I am not into rejection, so I don't think I will try that again. Maybe Jesus thinks like Patrick, not those others.

Jake is a big bear of a country guy. He is easy for anyone to talk with. He's a laid-back man full of common sense. I watch him use his dry humor on others. He mainly stays busy doing his own thing.

Performer has been trying to find a level of common ground with the others with no success. He has tried hard to understand and relate to them. He wanted so bad to be apart of them.

Several times I have looked over at him sitting alone watching the others. His head hung down alone listening to the others.

He has lost his pansy attitude and complaining.

I am going to make a great effort to help him with fitting in.

He was so glad to see me walking over to him. He asked, "something wrong?" I replied, "No I just wanted to talk awhile." He smiled as he said, "really that is great."

The darkness is all around now. Only a few stars are shining in the sky. You can see the rapid flashes of light from their bullets. You would think they were only equipped with machine guns.

I felt tension increase in me, and my heart raced. I need to approach each of the others both as individuals and as a group. I can see they are starting to get extremely upset as we are told to take cover.

I ended up with Patrick off to my right. Bad I had Yankee to my left. Patrick to my right wasn't bad but to have Yankee on my left is nothing short of terrible. At least, he could not talk and look through his scope at the same time.

A sudden cry out of one of ours almost did me in. He was only a few feet from me. He said, " I am not ready." The medic told him, "it is only a wound, not deadly." So he felt at ease.

It had calm down then I heard Yankee suddenly scream.

Patrick threw down his rifle as he ran to help Yankee.

Yankee the same guy who did everything to rub Patrick's face in the mud. I could hardly believe what I was seeing.

Patrick started praying for Jesus to spare Yankee. He even had tears as he prayed for him, amazing. You could hear and see it was honest, genuine.

The bullet hit a vital area. Patrick was asking, "Jesus to have mercy, to heal Yankee."

Yankee managed to get out one word, "why?"

Patrick replied, "Jesus died for you, who am I to hate you?"

Man, wow, He died for you. Who am I to hate you? Hit deep, real deep.

"Yankee Jesus does love you. I did Him the way you did me. I found His mercy still cared about me. That is how I was able to care about you."

Yankee had a few tears, and so did I.

If there is a Jesus than Patrick reflects Him. No doubt he relates a loving, merciful God.

I watched them as I tried to comprehend what I had seen and that I am now seeing.

I was finding it hard not to want the Jesus Patrick was giving me and the others.

What if I died never being shown the real Jesus?

Who really is this Jesus?

Yankee met Jesus as Patrick prayed with him. Patrick told him, "now your life is in the hands of a God who heals."

The medics came rushing Yankee to safety and medical care.

Through tears, Patrick looked up, waved his hand.

I heard him say, "thank you for saving, healing and making my enemy be at peace with both you and myself."

Patrick went on his way humming a tune.

The attacks have let up now. I was able to help care for the wounded. Also, I helped encourage many that they could and will make it. In their lives, words had wiped them out. Now words were strengthening them.

I was still thinking about what I had seen.

My eyes finally cleared enough to see the stars above me. It isn't close to daybreak yet.

Taking cover during the attacks have left their marks upon me. I have so many cuts and bruises scattered on me. My uniform is torn, muddy.

Why do I have to be here? What has driven me to fight for the freedom of others? I have done this most of my life. Maybe it is simply my destiny. Something has put this fight in me. It sure isn't what I would choose on my own. I would have chosen to lay on a hill with a gentle rain falling upon me. And I would watch a horse running free. A perfect romantic dinner, candles, beautiful music in the background. A winters night cuddle up in front of a fireplace. So many other nights I would have chosen then this type of night. Yet, for some reason, this is where I am. Through embracing others, I have been embraced. Maybe that is who I am?

I will not surrender nor give up, not ever. I must bring as many as I can through this with me.

I thought about a story a very elderly man told me long ago. The story often gave me strength.

I had gone to the park on a warm sunny day.

I noticed a very old man walking towards me. Such a curious sight. He looked like an old country guy. He was happily whistling a tune. I had to smile as I watched his effort to keep his movement going with his tune.

He didn't go to the empty park bench but chose to sit where I was.

He said, "my name is John and it is my honor to talk to you today." I had to laugh as he told me, "why it is a mighty fine day to tell you a story."

He had a friend named Tom. He daily sat at the bus stop in front of John's store. Tom watched the buses stop, gather people. Each time he would say, "I wish I could ride one and experience it. Just where do you think it's going? What things do you think those people are going to see?" Over and over Tom watched others do what he wanted so badly to do.

One day John got angry with Tom. He asked him, "then why don't you ride one?" Tom answered, "it takes a dime. I don't think I have one." John questioned his response. "have you tried to see if you do have it." Tom only replied, "because I don't think I have what it takes." John offered to give Tom the dime and help him, but Tom refused.

One day Tom didn't show up at the bus stop. John went looking for him.

Tom's brother said, "Tom had died." It was sad but also odd. He told John that his brother was holding so tight something in his hand. Tom told his brother, "I think I will use this dime and ride the bus today."

John looked seriously over at me and said, "Tom, had what it took all along to live his dream. You have what it takes within you to fulfill yours. Don't wait as long as Tom did before you realize; you have had it all along."

He got up, smiled, then told me, "I will be on my way now. Maybe one day I will see you again. I do hope so." He went on his way whistling his tune and trying to keep step with his tune.

I returned there many times but never saw him again. Maybe he was there that one time to give me the gift of his story and a laugh.

I suddenly heard a noise in the bushes. I took hold of my weapon. My heart racing as I aimed toward the bushes. I was ready to do whatever I had to.

It was Seth. He had been unfairly labeled, a coward. I know he had been beaten down his whole life than he ended up here. He looked so battle fatigued. He had tried to fight so long now he isn't mentally or physically strong.

Seth makes me think of an old boxer who had fought a hundred rounds non-stop. He needed to step out and get some rest from the fight. He hasn't been ever allowed that.

For some time now Seth has been at a breaking point. He knew he couldn't handle much more. A good guy who was worn out.

Who made up the stupid word coward or hero anyway? I bet they have never been in Seth's shoes. It makes me angry, the mean abuse.

I told Seth to lean back, rest, I had his back.

He was sitting with both hands on his head. He was shaking as he told me, "I couldn't sleep. It isn't just my body, but my mind keeps replaying it over and over." He started hitting his hands on his head and saying, "the sounds; images will not stop replaying in my head. It will not let me rest. I can't handle all this anymore."

Seth looked at me serious as he said, "these are humans beings hurting us without any justified reason. I have been forced to hurt them or be harmed. None of it has been right that I have to do such a thing."

Sadly enough he was right. We had no choice but fight back. Why were they giving us no choice but fight them, harm them? How could I reason away such a senseless thing?

I put my hand on his shoulder as I looked up. In anger, I asked God, "if you are real and actually care than help Seth, please. I need your help here."

I heard another sound coming from the bushes. My heart racing again. I got Seth safe and motion for him to be silent.

I thought to myself, pull yourself together and be calm. I knew I had to clear my head before I got Seth and myself wiped out.

It was the enemy ready to use their weapon for destruction. I stayed between them and Seth. The enemy has hurt him far too much already, not now. I will not let them do more damage now.

I was better with my weapon than they were with theirs. They fell unable to harm anyone else.

I look back at Seth he was rolled up with his hands clenching his head, trembling.

As I was trying to help Seth, one of the enemies partly got up with his weapon. Seth saw him and tried to protect me.

I threw myself over Seth as I fired back and fully dealt with the enemy.

Seth wasn't physically wounded, but I was injured with a minor injury.

I told Seth, "wow you are a hero. If not for you we would have been wiped out. You put your fear aside to try and protect me."

Seth stopped trembling as he looked at me with deep thought and shock.

I added to Seth, "you are not a coward but a hero. I am going to tell others that also."

I helped him to his feet.

The others were not far off. As we walked up, they saw my injury.

With Seth at my side, I told them, "if not for Seth we would have been horribly wounded. He saved the night."

Seth still in shock kept looking at me. He was still trying to understand how he went from being treated as a coward to a hero.

The others around us started slapping him on his shoulder saying, "great job Seth."

The heroes had to be the medics caring for the wounded. They couldn't carry their weapon in defense and the stretcher at the same time. They chose to care for others first and foremost.

Patrick was a vital medic with his prayer and encouragement. He used prayer and encouraging words as his weapon. His Jesus was his hero, no doubt.

I will never forget Patrick bent over Yankee. Between the medics and Patrick, a great number of lives have been saved.

I looked for James. I found him sitting like a zombie.

I worked my way over to him.

He sat in front of me lifeless. He had no response when I spoke to him. His eyes just stared, no response to anything. He was frozen, in shock.

I asked one of the men what happened?

He said, "a new small group finally showed up to assist us. One the guys knew James and his girlfriend."

"He told James she had gone back to her old boyfriend now. They were making wedding plans.

James grabbed the guy, shaking him, screaming your lying. She loves me.

The guy broke loose as he said, I am sorry man, but it is true.

James went to his knees on the ground crying than he became lifeless ever since. He has given up."

The man added. "I would give anything to hear him again."

I felt so sad for James being so broken hearted. I shook my head as I looked at him.

Why did that guy have to tell him now? Couldn't it wait? So very stupid. Some people can't wait to tell their story. Maybe this guy didn't realize James hung his life on her.

As I was in deep thought about James, a commotion started.

Oh man, it is Todd and Randal again. Those two self-righteous vicious Christians at it again. I have had enough of them. That did it. I am going to deal with them.

Todd was going after it with Bruce while Randal agitated the fight on. Bruce was cruel himself. What a fighting match. Their words were flying like bullets as they tried to damage the other.

I grabbed Todd while Patrick grabbed the other. Randal still would not shut up.

Bruce walked off after expressing his authority over them with a threat.

I let go of Todd as I screamed, "what is wrong with you two? You have been nothing short of vicious. You have cut down everyone even each other with verbal abuse. As if verbal abuse wasn't enough your actions are abusive.

I have had it with your self-righteous attitude.

You make this Jesus look like He has a split personality.

Why don't you know the same Jesus Patrick does?"

"I don't want anything to do with the Jesus you have shown me. No one else does either. He is cruel. You two are cruel.

Isn't there enough to fight all around us without us also having to fight you two?

You scream about abortion while you abort the baby Christians. Have the heart to scream as loud to help the wounded, broken who needs someone to care."

They walked away acting insulted by what I said.

I needed to take a walk to clear my head.

The attacks are still somewhat quiet.

Sunrise is getting closer.

Bruce walked by with his arrogant attitude. His head was leaned back in a pompous manner. He wanted to be saluted by me.

One of the men told me Bruce made them feel like they were at Custard's last stand.

He hasn't listened to anyone, especially Chase.

Chase had reached the point of knocking Bruce out several times. Good example, Bruce walked up to Chase demanding a ridiculous order be carried out. Bruce stood waiting for Chase to salute and say, "yes sir." Chase stood with one hand clinched in a fist at his side. His other hand sharply saluted than came down into a fist.

Wilson could pull rank on him if he were not so afraid of him. Fear keeps him supporting what he fears.

Wilson, well he is still pacing giving stupid orders. He says, "his orders are to keep everyone obedient," as if they were a dog.

Chase is busy taking care of everything while avoiding Bruce and Wilson. Chase had intervened against orders, saving many lives.

I looked over and saw Performer. He had a small number of men engrossed in a story he was telling. He is such a character. I stopped to watch him. He is dramatic with an audience. He looks alright even in his tattered uniform. If his family saw him right now, we would need to revive them for sure.

I truly learned to like Performer. I even think of him as my friend. I hoped he makes it.

It must be a doozy of a story. His hands were moving every which way. I started laughing. He heard me and waved.

Josh is cleaning his rifle. He looked over at me. He said, "if your weapon is going to take care of you then you must take care of it."

Patrick was sitting to his right within his hands was his cross.

They both have their weapons against the enemy.

Josh has been mainly quiet. No one knows much about him especially his past. He doesn't let anyone in his space.

Josh said, "if you don't give anyone building blocks then they can not build a case against you." Made sense to me at the time.

I am so glad I never loved, well have been consumed by someone like James. He is still, out of it.

The attacks are increasing again. The cries of the wounded also have become intense. I felt like covering up my ears so I would not hear anyone else cry out. I knew in my heart; I could help only certain ones. The ones I couldn't help I didn't want to hear those. The ones who cried yet would not do what they needed to do, completely frustrated me. Their condition and life aren't just about them. Their loved ones also cried, often became frustrated. They couldn't help them make it through the battles. I understand far too well that kind of love.

Some people like Larry are in this not realizing what it actually is all about. Others are trying to con their way through this.

As the battles increased, Wilson totally lost it. No one could understand what he was saying. He started his pacing, shouting commands as the bullets were flying. We were able to ignore him until now. It sounded like he was commanding, "get up, forge forward." The rest he was saying, we couldn't understand. Against his will, we had to wrestle him down to keep him from being wounded. So sad, if only he had been allowed to be who he was meant to be. Maybe his outcome of this would have been different. I don't believe his family will understand it. It will be a shame to his family. The shame I felt was on his family, not on him.

Bruce got caught in a bad space. He had to take cover to protect himself. Which I must admit was really good to protect us from him. He sure couldn't be demanding undue respect where he ended up.

I had to laugh when one of our men said, "maybe we can pay the enemy to keep Bruce where he is. A person could get elbow problems from having to salute him continuously."

I assisted Chase reaching all we could with help and supplies. Each time I reached them, Patrick had been there before me praying. I honestly feel that Patrick's caring prayer was vital. I also believe it is why we were able to bring so many through.

I spotted Seth while caring for others. We sat and talked a short time about how he was doing.

Seth told me, "he didn't get it until he warned me about the enemy before he shot us. People have been wrong about who I am. I know now the difference."

I replied, "Seth, my prayer for you was answered. The so-called coward label was placed on you by people. I believe God allowed you see the truth within you. Everyone has had false labels placed on them. After so long it creates such a depressor to anyone's self-worth. Words can be deadly bullets flying, wounding the victim. I overcame the labels by knowing their label was not me. I didn't allow them to affect who I am inside."

"Seth, it is true the enemy are people we have to stand against. They are evil people wanting to destroy others to feed their cruelty. They gain their false sense of power by harming others.

We must stand against that type of people for the sake of the innocent victims."

"If you need me, Seth, I will be around. You know how to find me. I need to finish making my rounds. Stay strong and safe."

I looked back at Seth feeling good about how different of a sight he is now. I left Seth sitting calm, peaceful.

I am hoping I will reach James and find him alright.

When I reached James there, I found Patrick kneeled down praying.

Patrick raised his head then looked over at me.

I told him, "please go ahead and pray James back. I am going to check on the others."

Patrick said, "no please don't go. Pray with me for James. God does hear you also."

I stood still looking at Patrick than at James suspended in his mind. I walked over to them, kneeled down. I was not sure what good I could do with this praying thing.

Patrick patted my back. He said, "simply pray from your heart. God listens to the words or cries of our heart. Well, He also hears the tears that fall. God desires each of us to talk to Him no matter how we need to speak weather through a whisper, a thought or a shout."

"He loves us beyond even our need to be loved. He loves us with perfect love in our imperfection. It is hard to comprehend such love yet; it is real."

"He is wise enough to know you're not going to be instantly perfect. The journey He knows will be a step at a time."

I find no way to resist such words. I cannot resist with my mind nor with my heart.

Patrick prayed a true heartfelt prayer for James. That was great. I wasn't sure how to respond as he followed with a prayer for me.

I got up from my knees feeling awkward not knowing how to respond. Wow man, I was dealing with feelings I had never felt before.

The sun is starting to rise. Many made it through the night, others I need to check on.

I met up with Chase. He told me, "Larry was slightly wounded. It instantly made him so angry. He jumped up firing back as fast as he could. He fell due to that act of anger."

Chase said, "all of the others made it through. The sun is rising now. I need to get some rest."

"I agree rest is an amazing thought. I couldn't begin to tell you how tired I am."

I walked away only to stop and look up. I looked up at the heavens. The morning light is amazing.   The suns warmth felt great.

The sound of the birds singing, so beautiful. There are those who are being woke up by these very birds are complaining about it. I felt like singing with them.

The enemies threats were real. God's will for my life was stronger than any other.

My mind is beginning to clear. No one could imagine how fantastic was to say it is over for now. The glorious peace was the rainbow after the storm. I had survived.

I looked to my right there was a stream. I had not even noticed it before now. The stream was moving slow, easy. Strange the things you don't see when you are consumed with survival. In daylight, the peaceful things appear that the night hid.

One part of me kept reaching out to this Jesus. The other part of me was afraid.

I held in my hand the cross Patrick gave me. I felt a strange presence as if someone was staring at me. My awareness of the His presence grew stronger. I somehow knew He understood how I felt.

In the mist of natures beauty, I felt weak. In the presence of God, I felt humble, grateful. Feelings I have never felt before. As I realized the greatness of God's power, I fell to my knees and cried. "In this vast universe, why did God take time to care for someone as unimportant as me?"

NOW I CAN GO ON

Unto the wind, I cried, but it only blew on by.

Unto mankind, I looked up, but they only shrunk before my eyes.

Unto mankind, I cried out, but they were too busy to hear.

Unto God, I cried out; a voice returned, fear not I will never leave nor forsake you. Now let me dry your eyes. I do care.

My heart went at ease. My soul began to soar as I said thank you, God. I needed to know someone cared before I took another step. Now I can go on.

www.ingramcontent.com/pod-product-compliance
Lightning Source LLC
Chambersburg PA
CBHW071223130626
46555CB00004B/1828